COLOUR by NUMBERS

TIMES TABLES

CLAIRE STAMPER

Turn to page 96 for the Times Tables Facts!

ARCTURUS

ARCTURUS

This edition published in 2018 by Arcturus Publishing Limited
26/27 Bickels Yard, 151–153 Bermondsey Street,
London SE1 3HA

Copyright © Arcturus Holdings Limited

ISBN: 978-1-78828-515-5
CH006101NT
Supplier 29, Date 0518, Print run 6806

Written by Catherine Casey
Illustrated by Claire Stamper
Designed by Simon Oliver
Edited by Sebastian Rydberg

Printed in China

How to use this book

 This book is packed with fun colour-by-number puzzles, which will help you to learn multiplication and division.

 Choose one of the problems in a white area of the picture. What is the solution? Find your answer in the colouring key beneath the picture.

 The colour shown in the box matching your solution is the colour you must use to fill in that part of the picture.

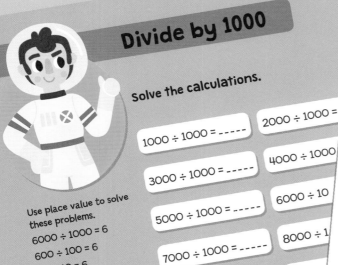

Divide by 1000

Solve the calculations.

$1000 ÷ 1000 = $ -----

$2000 ÷ 1000 = $

$3000 ÷ 1000 = $ -----

$4000 ÷ 1000$

$5000 ÷ 1000 = $ -----

$6000 ÷ 10$

$7000 ÷ 1000 = $ -----

$8000 ÷ 1$

$9000 ÷ 1000 = $ -----

10000

Use place value to solve these problems.

$6000 ÷ 1000 = 6$
$600 ÷ 100 = 6$
$60 ÷ 10 = 6$
$6 ÷ 1 = 6$

Or use the inverse operation (multiplication).

$1000 × 6 = 6000$
$6000 ÷ 1000 = 6$
$1000 × 4 = 4000$
$4000 ÷ 1000 = 4$

Learn how to solve multiplication and division problems before you start to colour!

After finishing the whole picture, check that it matches the **solution** at the back of the book.

Alien encounter

We come in peace! Complete this space scene by following the key at the bottom of the page.

Doubles

Two of them!

Doubling is when you have two lots of a number.

Add together two numbers that are the same.

For example 4 + 4 = 8.

$$\bullet\bullet\ +\ \bullet\bullet$$
$$\bullet\bullet\ \quad\ \bullet\bullet$$

Can you learn the doubles to 10?

Double 6 = _ _ _ _

Double 3 = _ _ _ _

Double 2 = _ _ _ _

Double 4 = _ _ _ _

Double 7 = _ _ _ _

Double 5 = _ _ _ _

Double 1 = _ _ _ _

Double 0 = _ _ _ _

Double 8 = _ _ _ _

Double 9 = _ _ _ _

Under the sea

Look at the seahorses swimming around! Use the key below to complete this underwater scene.

Double 9 = ?

Double 2 = ?

Double 5 = ?

Double 6 = ?

Double 4 = ?

Double 1 = ?

Double 8 = ?

Double 0 = ?

Double 3 = ?

Double 7 = ?

| 0 | 2 | 4 | 6 | 8 | 10 | 12 | 14 | 16 | 18 |

Halves

Find the answers by sharing each number into two equal groups.

Half of 4 = _ _ _ _ _

Half of 6 = _ _ _ _ _

½ of 8 = _ _ _ _ _

½ of 10 = _ _ _ _ _

Half of 2 = _ _ _ _ _

Half of 12 = _ _ _ _ _

½ of 14 = _ _ _ _ _

Half of 20 = _ _ _ _ _

Half of 18 = _ _ _ _ _

½ of 16 = _ _ _ _ _

Finding half!

We can write half as ½.

To find half of a number you need to share it equally into two.

For example, half of six = 6 shared by 2.

Half of six = 3.

Fairies and gnomes

Finish the woodland picture by using the key below to complete the scene. How many toadstools can you spot?

Half of 6 = ?

Half of 20 = ?

Half of 12 = ?

Half of 18 = ?

Half of 2

Half of 16 = ?

Half of 14 = ?

Half of 4 = ?

Half of 10 = ?

Half of 8 = ?

1 2 3 4 5 6 7 8 9 10

Two times table!

When you multiply 2 by a number, you need that number of groups of 2.

2 x 4 = 2, four times

2 + 2 + 2 + 2 = ?

2, 4, 6, 8

2 x 4 = 8.

Work out the **answers** by counting in twos.

2 x 12 = _____

2 x 10 = _____

2 x 8 = _____

2 x 5 = _____

2 x 11 = _____

2 x 1 = _____

2 x 0 = _____

2 x 6 = _____

2 x 2 = _____

2 x 7 = _____

Visit the lighthouse

Can you make the lighthouse shine brightly? Use the answers to the calculations to work out how to decorate this coastal scene.

Divide by two

Find the answers by sharing each number into two equal groups.

$12 \div 2 =$ _ _ _ _ _

$8 \div 2 =$ _ _ _ _ _

$10 \div 2 =$ _ _ _ _ _

$4 \div 2 =$ _ _ _ _ _

$2 \div 2 =$ _ _ _ _ _

$6 \div 2 =$ _ _ _ _ _

$14 \div 2 =$ _ _ _ _ _

$20 \div 2 =$ _ _ _ _ _

$18 \div 2 =$ _ _ _ _ _

$22 \div 2 =$ _ _ _ _ _

Divided means "shared by."

Dividing by two is the same as halving.

You need to share the number into two equal groups.

Remember the groups must be equal.

Fruit bowl

Have you had your daily serving of fruit? Use the answers to the calculations to complete the fruit bowl.

Ten times table

When you multiply 10 by a number, you need that number of groups of 10.

10 x 3 = 10, three times

10 + 10 + 10.

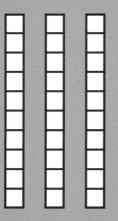

10, 20, 30

10 x 3 = 30.

Try counting in tens to find the answers!

10 x 11 = _ _ _ _ _

10 x 2 = _ _ _ _ _

10 x 0 = _ _ _ _ _

10 x 10 = _ _ _ _ _

10 x 3 = _ _ _ _ _

10 x 7 = _ _ _ _ _

10 x 6 = _ _ _ _ _

10 x 1 = _ _ _ _ _

10 x 4 = _ _ _ _ _

10 x 5 = _ _ _ _ _

Come to the magic show!

Abracadabra! Brighten up the magic show by following the key below.

0	10	20	30	40	50	60	70	100	110

Divide by ten

Use the ten times table to find the answers.

$120 \div 10 = 12$

$30 \div 10 = 3$

$70 \div 10 = 7$

$90 \div 10 = 9$

$60 \div 10 = 6$

$80 \div 10 = 8$

$10 \div 10 = 1$

$110 \div 10 = 11$

$20 \div 10 = 2$

$40 \div 10 = 4$

The opposite of multiplying is dividing.

You can use your knowledge of the ten times table to solve these division questions.
$10 \times 3 = 30$, so $30 \div 10 = 3$.

What multiplication fact could you use to solve:
$70 \div 10 = \_\_\_\_\_$?

$10 \times \_\_\_\_\_ = 70$.

At the water hole

The animals have gathered at the water hole. Complete the scene by using the key below.

1   2   3   4   6   7   8   9   10   12

Five times table

Can you count in fives?

5, 10, 15, 20, 25, 30, 35, 40, 45, 50, 55, 60.

5 x 3 is the same as 5 + 5 + 5.

Use repeated addition to find the answers.

5 x 12 = _ _ _ _

5 x 2 = _ _ _ _

5 x 3 = _ _ _ _

5 x 11 = _ _ _ _

5 x 5 = _ _ _ _

5 x 10 = _ _ _ _

5 x 8 = _ _ _ _

5 x 9 = _ _ _ _

5 x 3 = _ _ _ _

5 x 4 = _ _ _ _

A day trip to the zoo

Complete the picture of the zoo using the key below.
How many animals can you spot?

10 | 15 | 20 | 25 | 40 | 45 | 50 | 55 | 60

Divide by five

Use the five times table to find the **answers**.

30 ÷ 5 = _ _ _ _ _

45 ÷ 5 = _ _ _ _ _

60 ÷ 5 = _ _ _ _ _

20 ÷ 5 = _ _ _ _ _

35 ÷ 5 = _ _ _ _ _

25 ÷ 5 = _ _ _ _ _

15 ÷ 5 = _ _ _ _ _

10 ÷ 5 = _ _ _ _ _

50 ÷ 5 = _ _ _ _ _

55 ÷ 5 = _ _ _ _ _

The opposite of multiplying is dividing.

You can use your knowledge of the five times table to solve these division questions.

5, 10, 15, 20, 25, 30, 35, 40, 45, 50, 55, 60.

5 x 3 = 15, so 15 ÷ 5 = 3.

What multiplication fact could you use to solve:

30 ÷ 5 = _ _ _ _ _ ?

5 x _ _ _ _ _ = 30.

A treasure chest of toys

What toys can you spot in the toy box? Shade in the rest of the picture by using the key below.

The three times table

Try counting in threes:

3, 6, 9, 12, 15, 18, 21, 24, 27, 30, 33, 36.

3 x 4 is the same as 3 + 3 + 3 + 3.

3, 6, 9, 12

Use repeated addition to find the answers.

3 x 3 = _ _ _ _

3 x 4 = _ _ _ _

3 x 12 = _ _ _ _

3 x 7 = _ _ _ _

3 x 6 = _ _ _ _

3 x 10 = _ _ _ _

3 x 0 = _ _ _ _

3 x 5 = _ _ _ _

3 x 11 = _ _ _ _

3 x 1 = _ _ _ _

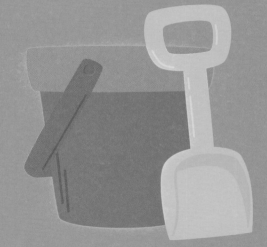

A day at the seaside

Sun, sand, sea, and a picnic. Let's hope they don't get sand in their sandwiches! Shade in the picture using the key below.

| 0 | 3 | 9 | 12 | 15 | 18 | 21 | 30 | 33 | 36 |

Divide by three

Use the three times table to find the answers.

9 ÷ 3 = _ _ _ _ _

12 ÷ 3 = _ _ _ _ _

36 ÷ 3 = _ _ _ _ _

21 ÷ 3 = _ _ _ _ _

18 ÷ 3 = _ _ _ _ _

30 ÷ 3 = _ _ _ _ _

15 ÷ 3 = _ _ _ _ _

33 ÷ 3 = _ _ _ _ _

3 ÷ 3 = _ _ _ _ _

6 ÷ 3 = _ _ _ _ _

The opposite of multiplying is dividing.

You can use your knowledge of the three times table to solve these division questions.

3, 6, 9, 12, 15, 18, 21, 24, 27, 30, 33, 36.

3 x 6 = 18, so 18 ÷ 3 = 6.

What multiplication fact could you use to solve:

12 ÷ 3 = _ _ _ _ _ ?

3 x _ _ _ _ _ = 12.

Canoeing on the river

These friends are having fun, splashing around on the river. Fill in the rest of the picture using the key below.

The four times table

Double and double again to multiply by four. For example:

4 x 5 = _ _ _ _ _

You know double 5 = 10.

And double 10 = 20.

4 x 5 = 20.

4 x 8 = _ _ _ _ _

You know double 8 = 16.

And double 16 = 32.

4 x 8 = 32.

Double and double again to calculate the answers.

4 x 5 = _ _ _ _ _

4 x 8 = _ _ _ _ _

4 x 7 = _ _ _ _ _

4 x 2 = _ _ _ _ _

4 x 0 = _ _ _ _ _

4 x 11 = _ _ _ _ _

4 x 9 = _ _ _ _ _

4 x 10 = _ _ _ _ _

4 x 3 = _ _ _ _ _

4 x 4 = _ _ _ _ _

Fun on the water

Look at the people zooming around on the water. Finish the picture by using the key below, and the answers to the calculations.

| 0 | 8 | 12 | 16 | 20 | 28 | 32 | 36 | 40 | 44 |

Divide by four

Halve and halve again to calculate the answers.

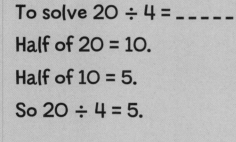

Halve and halve again.
For example:
To solve $20 \div 4 =$ _ _ _ _ _
Half of 20 = 10.
Half of 10 = 5.
So $20 \div 4 = 5$.

$32 \div 4 =$ _ _ _ _ _

$28 \div 4 =$ _ _ _ _ _

$8 \div 4 =$ _ _ _ _ _

$44 \div 4 =$ _ _ _ _ _

$36 \div 4 =$ _ _ _ _ _

$40 \div 4 =$ _ _ _ _ _

$12 \div 4 =$ _ _ _ _ _

$16 \div 4 =$ _ _ _ _ _

$4 \div 4 =$ _ _ _ _ _

$20 \div 4 =$ _ _ _ _ _

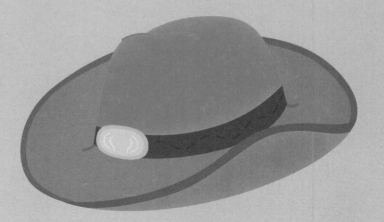

Yee-haw!

Fill in the cowgirl and cowboy scene by using the key below, once you have solved the calculations.

The six times table

Can you count in sixes?

6, 12, 18, 24, 30, 36, 42, 48, 54, 60, 66, 72.

What patterns can you spot?

$6 \times 3 = 6 + 6 + 6 = 18$.

Use repeated addition to find the answers.

6 x 4 = _ _ _ _ _

6 x 3 = _ _ _ _ _

6 x 7 = _ _ _ _ _

6 x 8 = _ _ _ _ _

6 x 6 = _ _ _ _ _

6 x 10 = _ _ _ _ _

6 x 12 = _ _ _ _ _

6 x 11 = _ _ _ _ _

6 x 2 = _ _ _ _ _

6 x 1 = _ _ _ _ _

Magical unicorns

Is there a pot of gold at the end of the rainbow? Finish the picture by using the key below, and the answers to the calculations.

6 x 1 = ?
6 x 4 = ?
6 x 3 = ?
6 x 7 = ?
6 x 8 = ?
6 x 6 = ?
6 x 10 = ?
6 x 2 = ?
6 x 12 = ?
6 x 11 = ?

| 6 | 12 | 18 | 24 | 36 | 42 | 48 | 60 | 66 | 72 |

Divide by Six

Find the answers by sharing the number into six equal groups.

24 ÷ 6 = _ _ _ _ _

18 ÷ 6 = _ _ _ _ _

42 ÷ 6 = _ _ _ _ _

48 ÷ 6 = _ _ _ _ _

36 ÷ 6 = _ _ _ _ _

60 ÷ 6 = _ _ _ _ _

72 ÷ 6 = _ _ _ _ _

66 ÷ 6 = _ _ _ _ _

12 ÷ 6 = _ _ _ _ _

6 ÷ 6 = _ _ _ _ _

Divided means "shared by."

You need to share the number into six equal groups.

Remember the groups must be equal.

Growing the crops

Can the scarecrows scare away the birds to stop them eating all the vegetables?
Complete the picture by using the key below.

The seven times table

You can draw an array (a row of objects to help you count) to help you solve multiplication calculations:

$$7 \times 3 = 7 + 7 + 7 = ?$$

7   14   21

These three rows of dots is an array.

There are 21 dots.

$$7 \times 3 = 21$$

Draw an array to find the answer to each calculation.

7 x 7 = _ _ _ _

7 x 3 = _ _ _ _

7 x 10 = _ _ _ _

7 x 2 = _ _ _ _

7 x 9 = _ _ _ _

7 x 12 = _ _ _ _

7 x 1 = _ _ _ _

7 x 0 = _ _ _ _

7 x 4 = _ _ _ _

7 x 8 = _ _ _ _

Kick off!

This looks like a fun game! Complete the match picture by using the key below.

| 0 | 7 | 14 | 21 | 28 | 49 | 56 | 63 | 70 | 84 |

Divide by Seven

Find the answers by sharing the number into seven equal groups.

49 ÷ 7 = _____

21 ÷ 7 = _____

70 ÷ 7 = _____

14 ÷ 7 = _____

63 ÷ 7 = _____

84 ÷ 7 = _____

7 ÷ 7 = _____

42 ÷ 7 = _____

28 ÷ 7 = _____

56 ÷ 7 = _____

Divided means "shared by".

You need to share the number into seven equal groups.

Remember the groups must be equal.

Whoosh down the mountains

Look at the children having fun in the snow. Complete the picture by using the key below.

| 1 | 2 | 3 | 4 | 6 | 7 | 8 | 9 | 10 | 12 |

The eight times table

Let's try counting in eights . . .

8, 16, 24, 32, 40, 48, 56, 64, 72, 80, 88, 96.

Can you spot any patterns? The numbers in the eight times table are always even!

$8 \times 5 = 8 + 8 + 8 + 8 + 8 = 40$.

Use repeated addition to find the answers.

$8 \times 8 = \_\_\_\_\_$

$8 \times 3 = \_\_\_\_\_$

$8 \times 2 = \_\_\_\_\_$

$8 \times 1 = \_\_\_\_\_$

$8 \times 10 = \_\_\_\_\_$

$8 \times 5 = \_\_\_\_\_$

$8 \times 6 = \_\_\_\_\_$

$8 \times 7 = \_\_\_\_\_$

$8 \times 9 = \_\_\_\_\_$

$8 \times 4 = \_\_\_\_\_$

Visit the tropical island

Watch out for sharks and falling coconuts! Use the answers to the calculations to fill in the rest of the picture.

| 8 | 16 | 24 | 32 | 40 | 48 | 56 | 64 | 72 | 80 |

Divide by eight

Use the eight times table to find the answers.

64 ÷ 8 = _ _ _ _ _

24 ÷ 8 = _ _ _ _ _

16 ÷ 8 = _ _ _ _ _

8 ÷ 8 = _ _ _ _ _

80 ÷ 8 = _ _ _ _ _

40 ÷ 8 = _ _ _ _ _

48 ÷ 8 = _ _ _ _ _

56 ÷ 8 = _ _ _ _ _

72 ÷ 8 = _ _ _ _ _

32 ÷ 8 = _ _ _ _ _

The opposite of multiplying is dividing.

You can use your knowledge of the eight times table to solve these division questions.

8, 16, 24, 32, 40, 48, 56, 64, 72, 80, 88, 96.

8 x 6 = 48, so 48 ÷ 8 = 6.

What multiplication fact could you use to solve:

80 ÷ 8 = _ _ _ _ _ ?

8 x _ _ _ _ _ = 80.

Choose a book!

Scan the shelves for a good book and find a comfy cushion. Fill in the blanks by using the key below.

A good way to remember the nine times table is to use your hands!

For example, what is 9 x 6?

To solve this, hold up all 10 fingers, and bend the 6th finger. To the left of your bent finger are 5 fingers (5 tens), and to the right are 4 fingers (4 units).

The answer is 54!

Use this method to solve these problems.

9 x 7 = _ _ _ _ _

9 x 9 = _ _ _ _ _

9 x 10 = _ _ _ _ _

9 x 1 = _ _ _ _ _

9 x 0 = _ _ _ _ _

9 x 4 = _ _ _ _ _

9 x 6 = _ _ _ _ _

9 x 5 = _ _ _ _ _

9 x 11 = _ _ _ _ _

9 x 12 = _ _ _ _ _

Walking in the hills

Discover the flowers, rocks, and paths on these hills. Use the key below to finish the picture.

Divide by nine

Use the nine times table to find the answers.

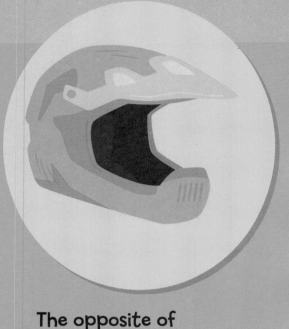

108 ÷ 9 = _ _ _ _ _

99 ÷ 9 = _ _ _ _ _

45 ÷ 9 = _ _ _ _ _

54 ÷ 9 = _ _ _ _ _

36 ÷ 9 = _ _ _ _ _

9 ÷ 9 = _ _ _ _ _

90 ÷ 9 = _ _ _ _ _

81 ÷ 9 = _ _ _ _ _

63 ÷ 9 = _ _ _ _ _

18 ÷ 9 = _ _ _ _ _

The opposite of multiplying is dividing.

You can use your knowledge of the nine times table to solve these division questions.

9, 18, 27, 36, 45, 54, 63, 72, 81, 90, 99, 108.

9 x 4 = 36, so 36 ÷ 9 = 4.

What multiplication fact could you use to solve:

54 ÷ 9 = _ _ _ _ _ ?

9 x _ _ _ _ _ = 54.

Pedal power

Look at the children having fun on their bikes! Finish the picture by using the key below.

$81 \div 9 = ?$

$63 \div 9 = ?$

$9 \div 9 = ?$

$54 \div 9 = ?$

$36 \div 9 = ?$

$90 \div 9 = ?$

$18 \div 9 = ?$

$45 \div 9 = ?$

$99 \div 9 = ?$

$108 \div 9 = ?$

| 1 | 2 | 4 | 5 | 6 | 7 | 9 | 10 | 11 | 12 |

The eleven times table

11, 22, 33, 44, 55, 66, 77, 88, 99, 110, 121, 132 . . .

Can you spot the pattern up to 99?

When you multiply 11 by a single digit, the tens and units in the answer match that digit.

11 x 5 = 55.

Use this pattern to help you solve the problems.

11 x 1 = _ _ _ _ _

11 x 2 = _ _ _ _ _

11 x 3 = _ _ _ _ _

11 x 4 = _ _ _ _ _

11 x 5 = _ _ _ _ _

11 x 6 = _ _ _ _ _

11 x 7 = _ _ _ _ _

11 x 8 = _ _ _ _ _

11 x 9 = _ _ _ _ _

11 x 10 = _ _ _ _ _

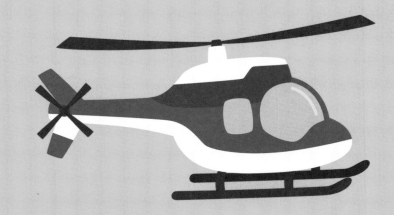

Up, up, and away!

Look at the helicopter up above the city. Use the key below to fill in the blanks.

Divide by eleven

Use the eleven times table to find the answers.

$110 \div 11 =$ _ _ _ _ _

$99 \div 11 =$ _ _ _ _ _

$88 \div 11 =$ _ _ _ _ _

$77 \div 11 =$ _ _ _ _ _

$66 \div 11 =$ _ _ _ _ _

$55 \div 11 =$ _ _ _ _ _

$44 \div 11 =$ _ _ _ _ _

$33 \div 11 =$ _ _ _ _ _

$22 \div 11 =$ _ _ _ _ _

$11 \div 11 =$ _ _ _ _ _

The opposite of multiplying is dividing.

You can use your knowledge of the eleven times table to solve these division questions.

11, 22, 33, 44, 55, 66, 77, 88, 99, 110, 121, 132.

$11 \times 3 = 33$, and $33 \div 11 = 3$.

What multiplication fact could you use to solve:

$88 \div 11 =$ _ _ _ _ _ ?

$11 \times$ _ _ _ _ _ $= 88$.

Fairy tale castle

Explore the beautiful castle. Can you spot the croaky frog? Use the answers to the calculations to work out how to fill in the blanks.

1   2   3   4   5   7   8   9   10   11

The twelve times table

12, 24, 36, 48, 60, 72, 84, 96, 108, 120, 132, 144.

Multiply by the tens first, then the units, and add them together. For example:

12 x 3 = _ _ _ _ _?

10 x 3 = 30.

2 x 3 = 6.

30 + 6 = 36.

Use this method to solve the calculations.

12 x 5 = _ _ _ _

12 x 3 = _ _ _ _

12 x 10 = _ _ _ _

12 x 11 = _ _ _ _

12 x 1 = _ _ _ _

12 x 6 = _ _ _ _

12 x 9 = _ _ _ _

12 x 12 = _ _ _ _

12 x 4 = _ _ _ _

12 x 8 = _ _ _ _

A day at the beach

Complete this picture of a fun day at the beach by following the key below.

| 12 | 36 | 48 | 60 | 72 | 96 | 108 | 120 | 132 | 144 |

Divide by twelve

Use the twelve times table to find the **answers.**

$60 \div 12 =$ _ _ _ _ _

$36 \div 12 =$ _ _ _ _ _

$120 \div 12 =$ _ _ _ _ _

$132 \div 12 =$ _ _ _ _ _

$12 \div 12 =$ _ _ _ _ _

$72 \div 12 =$ _ _ _ _ _

$108 \div 12 =$ _ _ _ _ _

$144 \div 12 =$ _ _ _ _ _

$48 \div 12 =$ _ _ _ _ _

$96 \div 12 =$ _ _ _ _ _

The opposite of dividing is multiplying.

You can use your knowledge of the twelve times table to solve these division questions.

12, 24, 36, 48, 60, 72, 84, 96, 108, 120, 132, 144.

$12 \times 3 = 36$, and $36 \div 12 = 3$.

What multiplication fact could you use to solve:

$60 \div 12 =$ _ _ _ _ _ ?

$12 \times$ _ _ _ _ _ $= 60$.

Swimming with turtles

Discover the fantastic things under the sea. Use the key below to complete the picture.

Divide and multiply-twos

Look carefully at the symbol. Some of the problems are multiplying, and some are dividing!

Remember . . .

Dividing by 2 is the same as halving.

Multiplying by 2 is the same as doubling.

24 ÷ 2 = 12.

12 x 2 = 24.

Double and halve to find the answers to these problems.

6 x 2 = _ _ _ _ _

7 x 2 = _ _ _ _ _

5 x 2 = _ _ _ _ _

11 x 2 = _ _ _ _ _

12 x 2 = _ _ _ _ _

18 ÷ 2 = _ _ _ _ _

20 ÷ 2 = _ _ _ _ _

16 ÷ 2 = _ _ _ _ _

10 ÷ 2 = _ _ _ _ _

14 ÷ 2 = _ _ _ _ _

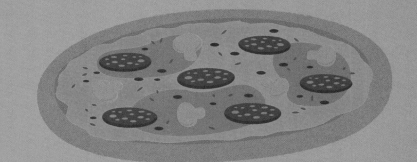

Let's make a pizza!

Yummy, yummy! The chefs are busy baking in the kitchen. Complete the picture by using the key below.

Divide and multiply tens

Solve these mixed dividing and multiplying problems using the ten times table.

Let's try counting in tens.

10, 20, 30, 40, 50, 60, 70, 80, 90, 100, 110, 120.

Remember that dividing is the opposite of multiplying.

Use the ten times table to help you.

10 x 6 = 60.

60 ÷ 10 = 6.

10 x 6 = _ _ _ _ _

10 x 10 = _ _ _ _ _

10 x 5 = _ _ _ _ _

10 x 8 = _ _ _ _ _

10 x 7 = _ _ _ _ _

110 ÷ 10 = _ _ _ _ _

70 ÷ 10 = _ _ _ _ _

80 ÷ 10 = _ _ _ _ _

30 ÷ 10 = _ _ _ _ _

90 ÷ 10 = _ _ _ _ _

Let's go and fly a kite!

Complete this picture of these cute kites by solving the problems, and following the key below.

Divide and multiply fives

Let's try counting in fives.

5, 10, 15, 20, 25, 30, 35, 40, 45, 50, 55, 60, 65, 70.

Remember dividing is the opposite of multiplying.

Use the five times table to help you.

$5 \times 6 = 30$.

$30 \div 5 = 6$.

Solve these mixed dividing and multiplying problems using the five times table.

$5 \times 8 = \_\_\_\_\_$

$35 \div 5 = \_\_\_\_\_$

$5 \times 9 = \_\_\_\_\_$

$50 \div 5 = \_\_\_\_\_$

$5 \times 4 = \_\_\_\_\_$

$30 \div 5 = \_\_\_\_\_$

$5 \times 2 = \_\_\_\_\_$

$10 \div 5 = \_\_\_\_\_$

$5 \times 11 = \_\_\_\_\_$

$60 \div 5 = \_\_\_\_\_$

Under the sea

Complete this underwater scene by using the key below. What could be hiding in the treasure chest?

Mix it up!

Can you complete the calculations by remembering the times table?

10 x 2 = _ _ _ _ _

10 x 7 = _ _ _ _ _

10 x 10 = _ _ _ _ _

2 x 5 = _ _ _ _ _

2 x 8 = _ _ _ _ _

2 x 6 = _ _ _ _ _

5 x 8 = _ _ _ _ _

5 x 9 = _ _ _ _ _

5 x 1 = _ _ _ _ _

5 x 11 = _ _ _ _ _

Read the questions carefully to find out if you need to count in twos, fives, or tens.

You can use repeated addition to help solve the problems, or you can remember the times tables facts.

2 x 4 = 4 + 4.

5 x 6 = 6 + 6 + 6 + 6 + 6.

10 x 8 = 8 + 8 + 8 + 8 + 8 + 8 + 8 + 8 + 8 + 8.

Fun in the rain

The children are having fun splashing in the puddles. Complete this wet weather scene by using the key below.

Threes, fours, and eights

Try to learn your times table facts.
How quickly can you recall them?

3, 6, 9, 12, 15, 18, 21, 24, 27, 30, 33, 36.

4, 8, 12, 16, 20, 24, 28, 32, 36, 40, 44, 48.

8, 16, 24, 32, 40, 48, 56, 64, 72, 80, 88, 96.

Can you spot any patterns?

Can you recall your times tables to solve these problems quickly?

3 x 4 = _ _ _ _ _

4 x 7 = _ _ _ _ _

8 x 2 = _ _ _ _ _

3 x 8 = _ _ _ _ _

4 x 10 = _ _ _ _ _

8 x 9 = _ _ _ _ _

3 x 3 = _ _ _ _ _

4 x 5 = _ _ _ _ _

8 x 8 = _ _ _ _ _

3 x 10 = _ _ _ _ _

Down under

Discover the plants, rocks, and animals in the Australian Outback. Use the key below to finish the picture.

4 x 5 = ?

8 x 2 = ?

3 x 4 = ?

4 x 10 = ?

4 x 7 = ?

15 x 2 = ?

3 x 8 = ?

3 x 10 = ?

3 x 3 = ?

8 x 8 = ?

| 9 | 12 | 16 | 20 | 24 | 28 | 30 | 40 | 64 |

Sixes, sevens, nines, elevens, and twelves

Can you recall your times tables to solve these problems quickly?

Test your knowledge of times table facts.

How quickly can you recall them?

6, 12, 18, 24, 30, 36, 42, 48, 54, 60, 66, 72.

7, 14, 21, 28, 35, 42, 49, 56, 63, 70, 77, 84.

9, 18, 27, 36, 45, 54, 63, 72, 81, 90, 99, 108.

11, 22, 33, 44, 55, 66, 77, 88, 99, 110, 121.

12, 24, 36, 48, 60, 72, 84, 96, 108, 120, 136.

Can you spot any patterns?

$6 \times 10 = \_\,\_\,\_\,\_$

$7 \times 10 = \_\,\_\,\_\,\_$

$9 \times 5 = \_\,\_\,\_\,\_$

$7 \times 6 = \_\,\_\,\_\,\_$

$11 \times 3 = \_\,\_\,\_\,\_$

$12 \times 8 = \_\,\_\,\_\,\_$

$6 \times 6 = \_\,\_\,\_\,\_$

$9 \times 6 = \_\,\_\,\_\,\_$

$11 \times 7 = \_\,\_\,\_\,\_$

$12 \times 2 = \_\,\_\,\_\,\_$

Land of the dinosaurs

Roar! Fill in these extinct creatures by using the key below.

24   33   36   42   45   54   60   70   77   96

Counting in hundreds

Can you count in hundreds?

100, 200, 300, 400, 500, 600, 700, 800, 900, 1000.

One method of solving multiplication problems is by repeated addition.

100 x 3 = 100 + 100 + 100 = 300.

Solve the problems by counting in hundreds.

100 x 2 = _ _ _ _

100 x 8 = _ _ _ _

100 x 5 = _ _ _ _

100 x 0 = _ _ _ _

100 x 10 = _ _ _ _

100 x 7 = _ _ _ _

100 x 3 = _ _ _ _

100 x 4 = _ _ _ _

100 x 6 = _ _ _ _

100 x 9 = _ _ _ _

Yo ho ho!

Let's set sail! Where do you think the pirate treasure might be? Fill in the blank sections using the key below.

Counting in fifties

Count in fifties to solve the problems.

50 x 2 = _ _ _ _

50 x 1 = _ _ _ _

50 x 0 = _ _ _ _

50 x 10 = _ _ _ _

50 x 3 = _ _ _ _

50 x 4 = _ _ _ _

50 x 5 = _ _ _ _

50 x 6 = _ _ _ _

50 x 7 = _ _ _ _

50 x 8 = _ _ _ _

Have a go at counting in fifties.

50, 100, 150, 200, 250, 300, 350, 400, 450, 500.

Can you spot the pattern?

50 x 4 = 50 + 50 + 50 + 50 = 200.

50, 100, 150, 200

Blast off!

Look at the spaceships zooming through space. Where are they are going?
Fill in the blank sections by using the key below.

Counting in twenty-fives

Have a go at counting in twenty-fives.

25, 50, 75, 100, 125, 150, 175, 200, 225, 250.

Can you see a pattern?

25 x 3 = 25 + 25 + 25 = 75.

Count in twenty-fives to solve the calculations.

25 x 0 = _ _ _ _ _

25 x 1 = _ _ _ _ _

25 x 2 = _ _ _ _ _

25 x 3 = _ _ _ _ _

25 x 4 = _ _ _ _ _

25 x 5 = _ _ _ _ _

25 x 6 = _ _ _ _ _

25 x 7 = _ _ _ _ _

25 x 8 = _ _ _ _ _

12 x 9 = _ _ _ _ _

Take the dog for a walk

Splish splash! Through the mud and over the hills, this family is walking their dogs. Complete the picture by using the key below to fill in the blanks.

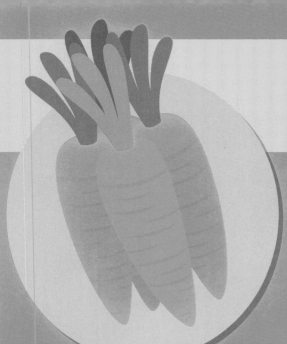

Counting in thousands

Count in thousands to solve these problems.

1000 x 0 = _ _ _ _ _

1000 x 1 = _ _ _ _ _

1000 x 2 = _ _ _ _ _

1000 x 3 = _ _ _ _ _

1000 x 4 = _ _ _ _ _

1000 x 5 = _ _ _ _ _

1000 x 6 = _ _ _ _ _

1000 x 7 = _ _ _ _ _

1000 x 8 = _ _ _ _ _

1000 x 9 = _ _ _ _ _

Let's try counting in thousands!

1000, 2000, 3000, 4000, 5000, 6000, 7000, 8000, 9000, 10000.

Have a go at counting aloud using different voices.

1000 x 4 = 1000 + 1000 + 1000 + 1000 = 4000.

Pet hutch

Look at these pets who are about to eat their meal. Complete the picture by using the key below.

0 1000 2000 3000 4000 5000 6000 7000 8000 9000

Multiplying multiples of ten

You can use known multiplication facts and place value to solve these problems.

For example, if you know $3 \times 5 = 15$, you can use this to solve $30 \times 5 = \_\_\_\_\_$ because $3 \times 10 = 30$. So you multiply both sides of the problem by 10.

$30 \times 5 = 15 \times 10$

$30 \times 5 = 150$

(3×10)

Hundreds	Tens	Units
	1	5
1	5	0

When you multiply by ten, 0 becomes a place holder and the digits move to the left. The number is ten times bigger.

If you know $7 \times 3 = 21$

then $70 \times 3 = 21 \times 10$

Hundreds	Tens	Units
	2	1
2	1	0

Use multiplication facts and place value to solve these problems.

$30 \times 5 = \_\_\_\_\_$

$20 \times 2 = \_\_\_\_\_$

$40 \times 3 = \_\_\_\_\_$

$80 \times 2 = \_\_\_\_\_$

$50 \times 3 = \_\_\_\_\_$

$60 \times 2 = \_\_\_\_\_$

$70 \times 3 = \_\_\_\_\_$

$10 \times 7 = \_\_\_\_\_$

$80 \times 5 = \_\_\_\_\_$

$20 \times 4 = \_\_\_\_\_$

Beautiful budgies

Fill in the feathers of these beautiful birds, sitting on a branch. Use the key below to work out the correct answers.

40 x 3 = ?

20 x 2 = ?

70 x 3 = ?

80 x 5 = ?

20 x 4 = ?

60 x 2 = ?

10 x 7 = ?

10 x 7 = ?

30 x 5 = ?

50 x 3 = ?

80 x 2 = ?

| 40 | 70 | 80 | 120 | 150 | 160 | 210 | 400 |

More multiplying

Use multiplication facts and place value to solve these problems.

90 x 2 = _180_   30 x 8 = _240_

40 x 4 = _160_   80 x 3 = _240_

60 x 5 = _300_   70 x 1 = _70_

10 x 9 = _90_   20 x 8 = _160_

20 x 5 = _100_   60 x 3 = _180_

Remember you can use multiplication facts and place value to solve these problems, for example:

2 x 8 = 16.

20 x 8 = 160.

8 x 3 = 24.

80 x 3 = 240.

Rock 'n' roll

What instruments can you spot the band members playing? Use the key below to work out the answers, and complete the picture.

70   90   100   160   180   240   300

Multiplying two-digit numbers

To multiply a two-digit number by a one-digit number, multiply the tens first, then the units, and finally add the totals together.

For example:

41 x 3 = _ _ _ _ _ ?

40 x 3 = 120.

1 x 3 = 3.

120 + 3 = 123.

To solve these problems, multiply the tens first, then the units, and finally add the totals together.

23 x 5 = _ _ _ _ _

46 x 2 = _ _ _ _ _

56 x 10 = _ _ _ _ _

72 x 2 = _ _ _ _ _

83 x 5 = _ _ _ _ _

25 x 5 = _ _ _ _ _

41 x 3 = _ _ _ _ _

54 x 4 = _ _ _ _ _

75 x 3 = _ _ _ _ _

65 x 2 = _ _ _ _ _

Lively lions

Can you see the lion cubs playing in the grass? Use the key below to work out the answers, and complete the picture.

| 92 | 115 | 123 | 125 | 130 | 144 | 216 | 225 | 415 | 560 |

Dividing by 100

Remember division is the inverse (or opposite) of multiplication.

4 x 100 = 400.

400 ÷ 100 = 4.

Use the inverse operation to solve these problems.

300 ÷ 100 = _____   400 ÷ 100 = _____   500 ÷ 100 = _____

900 ÷ 100 = _____   1000 ÷ 100 = _____   200 ÷ 100 = _____

600 ÷ 100 = _____   100 ÷ 100 = _____   700 ÷ 100 = _____

800 ÷ 100 = _____

The circus comes to town

Enter the big top tent to watch juggling and acrobatics. Fill in the blank sections by using the key below.

Divide by 1000

Solve the calculations.

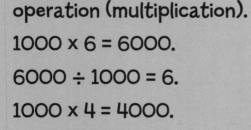

Use place value to solve these problems.

6000 ÷ 1000 = 6.

600 ÷ 100 = 6.

60 ÷ 10 = 6.

6 ÷ 1 = 6.

Or use the inverse operation (multiplication).

1000 x 6 = 6000.

6000 ÷ 1000 = 6.

1000 x 4 = 4000.

4000 ÷ 1000 = 4.

1000 ÷ 1000 = _ _ _ _ _

2000 ÷ 1000 = _ _ _ _ _

3000 ÷ 1000 = _ _ _ _ _

4000 ÷ 1000 = _ _ _ _ _

5000 ÷ 1000 = _ _ _ _ _

6000 ÷ 1000 = _ _ _ _ _

7000 ÷ 1000 = _ _ _ _ _

8000 ÷ 1000 = _ _ _ _ _

9000 ÷ 1000 = _ _ _ _ _

10000 ÷ 1000 = _ _ _ _ _

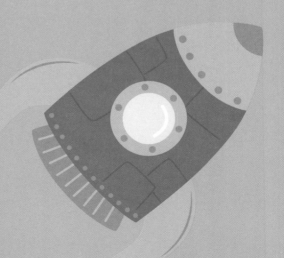

Alien encounter

We come in peace! Complete this space scene by following the key at the bottom of the page.

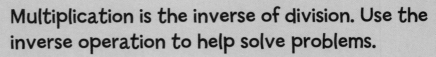

Dividing multiples of ten

Multiplication is the inverse of division. Use the inverse operation to help solve problems.

6 x 5 = 30.

30 ÷ 5 = 6.

Division means sharing into equal groups.

20 ÷ 4 = _ _ _ _ _ ?

Use your preferred method to solve the problems.

30 ÷ 5 = _ _ _ _ _

40 ÷ 2 = _ _ _ _ _

50 ÷ 5 = _ _ _ _ _

60 ÷ 6 = _ _ _ _ _

70 ÷ 2 = _ _ _ _ _

80 ÷ 4 = _ _ _ _ _

90 ÷ 10 = _ _ _ _ _

20 ÷ 4 = _ _ _ _ _

20 ÷ 5 = _ _ _ _ _

80 ÷ 2 = _ _ _ _ _

Time for tennis

A tennis match is in full swing. Fill in the blanks by using the key below.

$80 \div 2 = ?$

$30 \div 5 = ?$

$70 \div 2 = ?$

$80 \div 4 = ?$

$60 \div 6 = ?$

$70 \div 2 = ?$

$20 \div 4 = ?$

$20 \div 5 = ?$

$90 \div 10 = ?$

$50 \div 5 = ?$

$20 \div 4 = ?$

$40 \div 2 = ?$

| 4 | 5 | 6 | 9 | 10 | 20 | 35 | 40 |

Divide two-digits by one-digit

Multiplication is the opposite of division.

Use your knowledge of multiplication facts to help you solve these problems:

For example, if you know 9 x 7 = 63, then 63 ÷ 7 = 9.

Or share into equal groups, for example 84 shared into 4 equal groups:

21	21	21	21

84 ÷ 4 = 21.

Use your chosen method to solve these calculations.

92 ÷ 2 = _ _ _ _ _

48 ÷ 3 = _ _ _ _ _

63 ÷ 7 = _ _ _ _ _

84 ÷ 4 = _ _ _ _ _

95 ÷ 5 = _ _ _ _ _

45 ÷ 3 = _ _ _ _ _

68 ÷ 4 = _ _ _ _ _

84 ÷ 6 = _ _ _ _ _

64 ÷ 4 = _ _ _ _ _

51 ÷ 3 = _ _ _ _ _

Moving house

The removal van has arrived, and is loading up the boxes. Fill in the blanks by using the key below.

9   10   14   15   16   17   19   21   46

Mixed multiplication and division

Have a go at answering these mixed multiplication and division questions.

Use your times table knowledge.

Remember, multiplication is the inverse of division!

Use your chosen method to solve these calculations.

12 x 6 = _ _ _ _ _

5 x 7 = _ _ _ _ _

8 x 3 = _ _ _ _ _

18 ÷ 3 = _ _ _ _ _

49 ÷ 7 = _ _ _ _ _

10 x 9 = _ _ _ _ _

9 x 4 = _ _ _ _ _

70 ÷ 7 = _ _ _ _ _

2 x 2 = _ _ _ _ _

88 ÷ 8 = _ _ _ _ _

At the art studio

This artist is creating a painting. Can you help complete the picture by using the key below?

Solutions

4–5

Double 6 = 12
Double 3 = 6
Double 2 = 4
Double 4 = 8
Double 7 = 14
Double 5 = 10
Double 1 = 2
Double 0 = 0
Double 8 = 16
Double 9 = 18

10–11

12 ÷ 2 = 6
8 ÷ 2 = 4
10 ÷ 2 = 5
4 ÷ 2 = 2
2 ÷ 2 = 1
6 ÷ 2 = 3
14 ÷ 2 = 7
20 ÷ 2 = 10
18 ÷ 2 = 9
22 ÷ 2 = 11

6–7

Half of 4 = 2
Half of 6 = 3
Half of 8 = 4
Half of 10 = 5
Half of 2 = 1
Half of 12 = 6
Half of 14 = 7
Half of 20 = 10
Half of 18 = 9
Half of 16 = 8

12–13

10 x 11 = 110
10 x 2 = 20
10 x 0 = 0
10 x 10 = 100
10 x 3 = 30
10 x 7 = 70
10 x 6 = 60
10 x 1 = 10
10 x 4 = 40
10 x 5 = 50

8–9

2 x 12 = 24
2 x 10 = 20
2 x 8 = 16
2 x 5 = 10
2 x 11 = 22
2 x 1 = 2
2 x 0 = 0
2 x 6 = 12
2 x 2 = 4
2 x 7 = 14

14–15

120 ÷ 10 = 12
30 ÷ 10 = 3
70 ÷ 10 = 7
90 ÷ 10 = 9
60 ÷ 10 = 6
80 ÷ 10 = 8
10 ÷ 10 = 1
110 ÷ 10 = 10
20 ÷ 10 = 2
40 ÷ 10 = 4

16–17

5 x 12 = 60

5 x 2 = 10

5 x 3 = 15

5 x 11 = 55

5 x 5 = 25

5 x 10 = 50

5 x 8 = 40

5 x 9 = 45

5 x 3 = 15

5 x 4 = 20

22–23

9 ÷ 3 = 3

12 ÷ 3 = 4

36 ÷ 3 = 12

21 ÷ 3 = 7

18 ÷ 3 = 6

30 ÷ 3 = 10

15 ÷ 3 = 5

33 ÷ 3 = 11

3 ÷ 3 = 1

6 ÷ 3 = 2

18–19

30 ÷ 5 = 6

45 ÷ 5 = 9

60 ÷ 5 = 12

20 ÷ 5 = 4

35 ÷ 5 = 7

25 ÷ 5 = 5

15 ÷ 5 = 3

10 ÷ 5 = 2

50 ÷ 5 = 10

55 ÷ 5 = 11

24–25

4 x 5 = 20

4 x 8 = 32

4 x 7 = 28

4 x 2 = 8

4 x 0 = 0

4 x 11 = 44

4 x 9 = 36

4 x 10 = 40

4 x 3 = 12

4 x 4 = 16

20–21

3 x 3 = 9

3 x 4 = 12

3 x 12 = 36

3 x 7 = 21

3 x 6 = 18

3 x 10 = 30

3 x 0 = 0

3 x 5 = 15

3 x 11 = 33

3 x 1 = 3

26–27

32 ÷ 4 = 8

28 ÷ 4 = 7

8 ÷ 4 = 2

44 ÷ 4 = 11

36 ÷ 4 = 9

40 ÷ 4 = 10

12 ÷ 4 = 3

16 ÷ 4 = 4

4 ÷ 4 = 1

20 ÷ 4 = 5

28–29

6 x 4 = 24
6 x 3 = 18
6 x 7 = 42
6 x 8 = 48
6 x 6 = 36
6 x 10 = 60
6 x 12 = 72
6 x 11 = 66
6 x 2 = 12
6 x 1 = 6

34–35

49 ÷ 7 = 7
21 ÷ 7 = 3
70 ÷ 7 = 10
14 ÷ 7 = 2
63 ÷ 7 = 9
84 ÷ 7 = 12
7 ÷ 7 = 1
42 ÷ 7 = 6
28 ÷ 7 = 4
56 ÷ 7 = 8

30–31

24 ÷ 6 = 4
18 ÷ 6 = 3
42 ÷ 6 = 7
48 ÷ 6 = 8
36 ÷ 6 = 6
60 ÷ 6 = 10
72 ÷ 6 = 12
66 ÷ 6 = 11
12 ÷ 6 = 2
6 ÷ 6 = 1

36–37

8 x 8 = 64
8 x 3 = 24
8 x 2 = 16
8 x 1 = 8
8 x 10 = 80
8 x 5 = 40
8 x 6 = 48
8 x 7 = 56
8 x 9 = 72
8 x 4 = 32

32–33

7 x 7 = 49
7 x 3 = 21
7 x 10 = 70
7 x 2 = 14
7 x 9 = 63
7 x 12 = 84
7 x 1 = 7
7 x 0 = 0
7 x 4 = 28
7 x 8 = 56

38–39

64 ÷ 8 = 8
24 ÷ 8 = 3
16 ÷ 8 = 2
8 ÷ 8 = 1
80 ÷ 8 = 10
40 ÷ 8 = 5
48 ÷ 8 = 6
56 ÷ 8 = 7
72 ÷ 8 = 9
32 ÷ 8 = 4

40–41

9 x 7 = 63

9 x 9 = 81

9 x 10 = 90

9 x 1 = 9

9 x 0 = 0

9 x 4 = 36

9 x 6 = 54

9 x 5 = 45

9 x 11 = 99

9 x 12 = 108

46–47

110 ÷ 11 = 10

99 ÷ 11 = 9

88 ÷ 11 = 8

77 ÷ 11 = 7

66 ÷ 11 = 6

55 ÷ 11 = 5

44 ÷ 11 = 4

33 ÷ 11 = 3

22 ÷ 11 = 2

11 ÷ 11 = 1

42–43

108 ÷ 9 = 12

99 ÷ 9 = 11

45 ÷ 9 = 5

54 ÷ 9 = 6

36 ÷ 9 = 4

9 ÷ 9 = 1

90 ÷ 9 = 10

81 ÷ 9 = 9

63 ÷ 9 = 7

18 ÷ 9 = 2

48–49

12 x 5 = 60

12 x 3 = 36

12 x 10 = 120

12 x 11 = 132

12 x 1 = 12

12 x 6 = 72

12 x 9 = 108

12 x 12 = 144

12 x 4 = 48

12 x 8 = 96

44–45

11 x 1 = 11

11 x 2 = 22

11 x 3 = 33

11 x 4 = 44

11 x 5 = 55

11 x 6 = 66

11 x 7 = 77

11 x 8 = 88

11 x 9 = 99

11 x 10 = 110

50–51

60 ÷ 12 = 5

36 ÷ 12 = 3

120 ÷ 12 = 10

132 ÷ 12 = 11

12 ÷ 12 = 1

72 ÷ 12 = 6

108 ÷ 12 = 9

144 ÷ 12 = 12

48 ÷ 12 = 4

96 ÷ 12 = 8

52–53

6 x 2 = 12

7 x 2 = 14

5 x 2 = 10

11 x 2 = 22

12 x 2 = 24

18 ÷ 2 = 9

20 ÷ 2 = 10

16 ÷ 2 = 8

10 ÷ 2 = 5

14 ÷ 2 = 7

58–59

10 x 2 = 20

10 x 7 = 70

10 x 10 = 100

2 x 5 = 10

2 x 8 = 16

2 x 6 = 12

5 x 8 = 40

5 x 9 = 45

5 x 1 = 5

5 x 11 = 55

54–55

10 x 6 = 60

10 x 10 = 100

10 x 5 = 50

10 x 8 = 80

10 x 7 = 70

110 ÷ 10 = 11

70 ÷ 10 = 7

80 ÷ 10 = 8

30 ÷ 10 = 3

90 ÷ 10 = 9

60–61

3 x 4 = 12

4 x 7 = 28

8 x 2 = 16

3 x 8 = 24

4 x 10 = 40

8 x 9 = 72

3 x 3 = 9

4 x 5 = 20

8 x 8 = 64

3 x 10 = 30

56–57

5 x 8 = 40

35 ÷ 5 = 7

5 x 9 = 45

50 ÷ 5 = 10

5 x 4 = 20

30 ÷ 5 = 6

5 x 2 = 10

10 ÷ 5 = 2

5 x 11 = 55

60 ÷ 5 = 12

62–63

6 x 10 = 60

7 x 10 = 70

9 x 5 = 45

7 x 6 = 42

11 x 3 = 33

12 x 8 = 96

6 x 6 = 36

9 x 6 = 54

11 x 7 = 77

12 x 2 = 24

64–65

100 x 2 = 200
100 x 8 = 800
100 x 5 = 500
100 x 0 = 0
100 x 10 = 1000
100 x 7 = 700
100 x 3 = 300
100 x 4 = 400
100 x 6 = 600
100 x 9 = 900

70–71

1000 x 0 = 0
1000 x 1 = 1000
1000 x 2 = 2000
1000 x 3 = 3000
1000 x 4 = 4000
1000 x 5 = 5000
1000 x 6 = 6000
1000 x 7 = 7000
1000 x 8 = 8000
1000 x 9 = 9000

66–67

50 x 2 = 100
50 x 1 = 50
50 x 0 = 0
50 x 10 = 500
50 x 3 = 150
50 x 4 = 200
50 x 5 = 250
50 x 6 = 300
50 x 7 = 350
50 x 8 = 400

72–73

30 x 5 = 150
20 x 2 = 40
40 x 3 = 120
80 x 2 = 160
50 x 3 = 150
60 x 2 = 120
70 x 3 = 210
10 x 7 = 70
80 x 5 = 400
20 x 4 = 80

68–69

25 x 0 = 0
25 x 1 = 25
25 x 2 = 50
25 x 3 = 75
25 x 4 = 100
25 x 5 = 125
25 x 6 = 150
25 x 7 = 175
25 x 8 = 200
25 x 9 = 225

74–75

90 x 2 = 180
30 x 8 = 240
40 x 4 = 160
80 x 3 = 240
60 x 5 = 300
70 x 1 = 70
10 x 9 = 90
20 x 8 = 160
20 x 5 = 100
60 x 3 = 180

76–77

23 x 5 = 115

46 x 2 = 92

56 x 10 = 560

72 x 2 = 144

83 x 5 = 415

25 x 5 = 125

41 x 3 = 123

54 x 4 = 216

75 x 3 = 225

65 x 2 = 130

82–83

30 ÷ 5 = 6

40 ÷ 2 = 20

50 ÷ 5 = 10

60 ÷ 6 = 10

70 ÷ 2 = 35

80 ÷ 4 = 20

90 ÷ 10 = 9

20 ÷ 4 = 5

20 ÷ 5 = 4

80 ÷ 2 = 40

78–79

300 ÷ 100 = 3

400 ÷ 100 = 4

500 ÷ 100 = 5

900 ÷ 100 = 9

1000 ÷ 100 = 10

200 ÷ 100 = 2

600 ÷ 100 = 6

100 ÷ 100 = 1

700 ÷ 100 = 7

800 ÷ 100 = 8

84–85

92 ÷ 2 = 46

48 ÷ 3 = 16

63 ÷ 7 = 9

84 ÷ 4 = 21

95 ÷ 5 = 19

45 ÷ 3 = 15

68 ÷ 4 = 17

84 ÷ 6 = 14

64 ÷ 4 = 16

51 ÷ 3 = 17

80–81

1000 ÷ 1000 = 1

2000 ÷ 1000 = 2

3000 ÷ 1000 = 3

4000 ÷ 1000 = 4

5000 ÷ 1000 = 5

6000 ÷ 1000 = 6

7000 ÷ 1000 = 7

8000 ÷ 1000 = 8

9000 ÷ 1000 = 9

10000 ÷ 1000 = 10

86–87

12 x 6 = 72

5 x 7 = 35

8 x 3 = 24

18 ÷ 3 = 6

49 ÷ 7 = 7

10 x 9 = 90

9 x 4 = 36

70 ÷ 7 = 10

2 x 2 = 4

88 ÷ 8 = 11

Times Tables Facts

Trace your finger along the top yellow row until you find the first number in a problem. Then trace your finger downward until it lines up with the number on the yellow column that matches the second number in the problem. Your finger will be pointing to the solution!

	1	2	3	4	5	6	7	8	9	10	11	12
1	1	2	3	4	5	6	7	8	9	10	11	12
2	2	4	6	8	10	12	14	16	18	20	22	24
3	3	6	9	12	15	18	21	24	27	30	33	36
4	4	8	12	16	20	24	28	32	36	40	44	48
5	5	10	15	20	25	30	35	40	45	50	55	60
6	6	12	18	24	30	36	42	48	54	60	66	72
7	7	14	21	28	35	42	49	56	63	70	77	84
8	8	16	24	32	40	48	56	64	72	80	88	96
9	9	18	27	36	45	54	63	72	81	90	99	108
10	10	20	30	40	50	60	70	80	90	100	110	120
11	11	22	33	44	55	66	77	88	99	110	121	132
12	12	24	36	48	60	72	84	96	108	120	132	144

All the answers are called **multiples**. 72 is a multiple of 8 and 9.